MASTER ELK and the
MOUNTAIN LION

by JONATHAN LONDON

illustrated by

WAYNE McLOUGHLIN

AUTHOR'S NOTE

Tule (pronounced "TOO lee") elk, the smaller cousins of the Roosevelt and Rocky Mountain elk, once roamed in the hundreds of thousands along the coast of California and in the grasslands of the Central Valley. After gold was discovered, however, the tule elk were hunted almost to extinction. Some hid in the tule marshes. In 1875, a tule marsh on a rancher's land was drained. There he found what may have been the last of the tule elk—a single pair. With the protection of the state of California and the rancher who found them, the tule elk population slowly grew. Today, in various parts of central and coastal California where the tule elk have been reintroduced, they number close to 3,000.

To the memory of Julian Sotelo, who delighted in nature
and who was a natural delight —J. L.

For my daughter, Allison —W. M.

Published by Crown Publishers, Inc., a Random House company, 201 East 50th Street, New York, New York 10022

CROWN is a trademark of Crown Publishers, Inc.

Manufactured in Singapore

Library of Congress Cataloging-in-Publication Data
London, Jonathan, 1947–
Master Elk and the mountain lion / by Jonathan London :
illustrated by Wayne McLoughlin. — 1st ed.
p. cm.
Summary: A young tule elk grows up to become the master of his herd and defends it from the attack of a mountain lion.
1. Tule elk—Juvenile fiction. [1. Tule elk—Fiction. 2. Elk—Fiction. 3. Pumas—Fiction.] I. McLoughlin, Wayne, ill. II. Title.
PZ10.3.L8534Mas 1995
[Fic]—dc20 94-1754

ISBN 0-517-59917-1 (trade)
0-517-59918-X (lib. bdg.)

10 9 8 7 6 5 4 3 2 1   *First Edition*

Spring has come
and the tule elk have
shed their winter coats.
The nubs of new antlers
crop out on the bulls' heads,
and the cows move off
into a herd of their own.

One day, a pregnant cow strays
beyond the purple lupine
to the edge of a wild cliff
to be alone.

There, she gives birth
to a calf, speckled white.
He stands on wobbly legs
and forcefully nudges
for mother's milk.

Mother Elk keeps her eyes open,
on the lookout for danger.
There! On a nearby knoll,
a sleek young mountain lion
slinks through tall grass,
then crouches, ready to pounce.

Mother Elk stands between the lion
and her newborn calf. Beyond,
the cliff falls sheer to the sea.
Mother Elk calls in short, sharp barks
her warning,
and the rest of the herd flees.
The big cat leaps! Twenty-five feet
through the air . . .

And drags down a feeble old cow
who has straggled behind.
For now, Mother Elk
and her speckled calf
are safe.

Over the years,

Mountain Lion will prowl,

taking down weak or unwary elk.

Meanwhile, by the time he is four,

Mother Elk's calf has become a powerful young bull.

On a day at the end of summer,
the season of the rut begins.
It is the time when bull
challenges bull
to see who will mate
with the cows.

Young Bull feels so strong,
he steps up to do battle
with the leader of the herd.
As the red-winged blackbirds sing
O-ka-lay . . . o-ka-lee-onk,
he circles the old master . . .

and charges. They crash with a clatter
and lock antlers.
But the old master is too heavy
and throws Young Bull off balance.
Young Bull must wait
and grow stronger.

It's not for three more years
that he's big and powerful enough
to make a real challenge.
Now his huge rack spreads
like the branches of a tree,
and his chest and shoulders
are as thick as an oak.

The two mighty elk face off,
scrape their antlers
across the ground . . .

and charge!

This time Young Bull proves himself
the strongest and the swiftest,
and one by one, the new master
drives off all the other bulls.
His stare alone is enough
for most challengers.

Over the cold months,
Master Elk keeps close watch
over his harem of cows and their young.
Their coats grow heavy,
and the antlers on the bulls
drop to the earth
like weapons no longer needed.

Come spring, the tule elk
shed their winter coats,
and antlers again sprout
on the bulls' heads.

By summer, Master Elk's antlers are fully grown.
He has rubbed off the velvety skin,
and his rack bristles, shining and sharp
in the sun.

One day at dusk,
a mist drifts in,
and the scent of danger
fills the air.
From where he grazes above his herd,
Master Elk smells it.
His ears flatten.
He raises his head high:
it is the signal of warning.
The herd thunders away
toward the tall tule reeds
down by the bay.

But Master Elk stands his ground,
waiting for the slower, older cows
and young calves to find safety.
He looks around — and spies
the old cougar, crouched among boulders.

Mountain Lion's eyes
shine like emeralds
in the moon glow.

Suddenly — sure his herd is safe —
Master Elk *bolts!*
His hoofs pound the ground,
and quail flare from the scrubs
with a whoosh of wings.

The great cat
springs
from the rocks
and lands in the deep grass
where Master Elk stood.

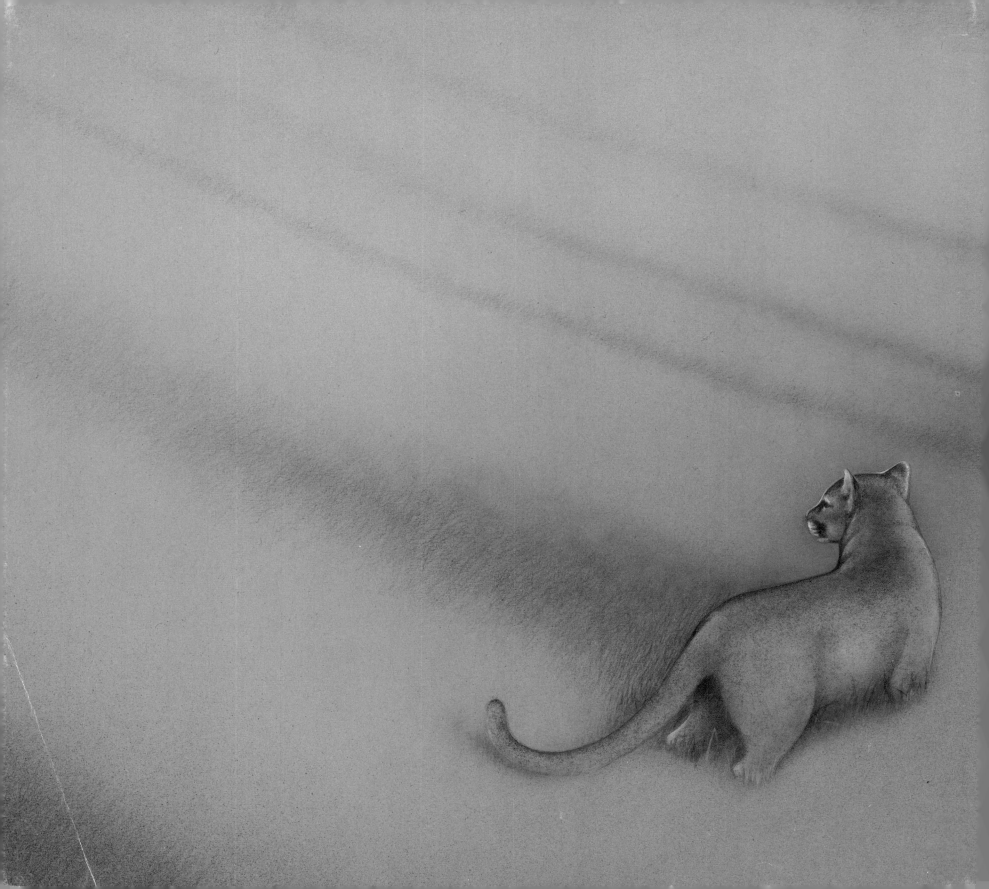

Mountain Lion rumbles and growls,
then flicks a huge paw
and licks it,
as if nothing in the world
has happened.

Swinging his long,
muscular body around,
he flows powerfully away
through the shadows.
There will be smaller game
for him tonight.

And Master Elk prances
down the low ridge
to rejoin his herd —
his majestic antlers
holding up the sky.